My Grandfather's Chest

The Magic Whistle

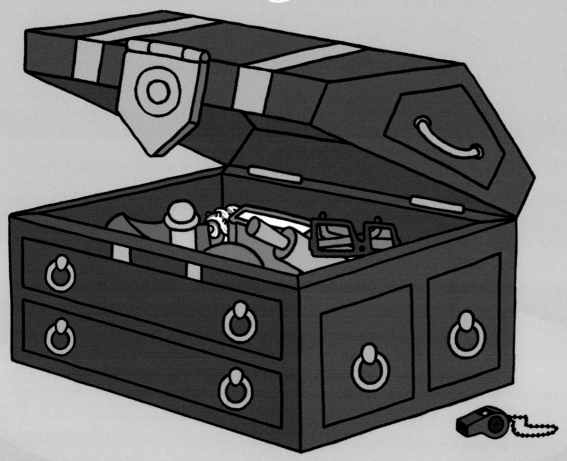

Brian McHarg

AuthorHouse™ UK
1663 Liberty Drive
Bloomington, IN 47403 USA
www.authorhouse.co.uk
UK TFN: 0800 0148641 (Toll Free inside the UK)
UK Local: 02036 956322 (+44 20 3695 6322 from outside the UK)

Because of the dynamic nature of the Internet, any web addresses or links contained in this book may have changed
since publication and may no longer be valid. The views expressed in this work are solely those of the author and do
not necessarily reflect the views of the publisher, and the publisher hereby disclaims any responsibility for them.

Any people depicted in stock imagery provided by Getty Images are models,
and such images are being used for illustrative purposes only.
Certain stock imagery © Getty Images.

This book is printed on acid-free paper.

ISBN: 978-1-7283-7557-1 (sc)
ISBN: 978-1-7283-7556-4 (e)

Print information available on the last page.

Published by AuthorHouse 09/21/2022

authorHOUSE®

My Grandfather's Chest

The Magic Whistle

Brian McHarg

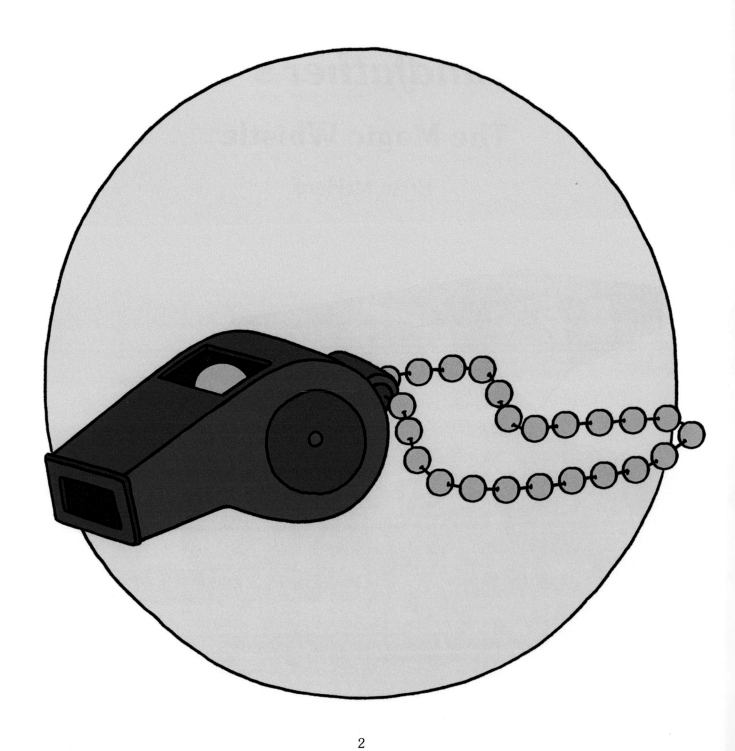

The Magic Whistle

Hello again! It's Paul. You must remember me by now!

I'll bet you've read my first two adventures already—the first one with the magic sunglasses and the second one with the magic seashell. If not, you should read both; I would love for you to enjoy them.

Anyway, I'm back again with a new magic adventure just for you! This one is even more unbelievable. Just read this new story and prepare to be amazed!

I was going through my grandfather's chest in my bedroom to see what else I could find—something else that might also be able to work magic!

I found a small grey whistle with a little dry pea inside it. I took it out and blew it.

It didn't make much of a sound, and nothing seemed to happen.

Or so I first thought …

One of my cats was on the floor beside my bed cleaning herself. This one was Jessica, the black one. When she isn't sleeping, she spends a lot of time licking her fur. She does keep herself spotlessly clean, I must say.

Anyway, I looked down at her and had a shock.

She was stuck, motionless, with one of her back legs up in the air and her rough tongue sticking out.

She wasn't moving at all; she was just frozen!

I stroked her, but she didn't move an inch.

As I glanced up, I saw a bird flying past my window.

I say flying, but it wasn't.

It wasn't moving.

It was frozen in midair—motionless, just like the cat.

I blew the whistle again; immediately, Jessica resumed her cleaning routine, and the bird flew on.

This surely was a magic whistle.

It could make time seem to stand still.

5

Breakfast and Some Good News

Suddenly, I became aware that Mummy was repeatedly calling me.

"Come on, Paul; breakfast is ready," she shouted.

I ran downstairs to find my brother, William, already tucking into a huge bowl of Rice Krispies.

I think he is very greedy with food; that is why he is quite fat, although Mummy describes him as just chubby.

Mummy exclaimed, "I've been calling you for ten minutes. You seem to be in a daze these days; I don't know what has got into you."

I said I was sorry and told her I hadn't heard with my bedroom door closed. (It wasn't actually; I was just busy trying out the whistle, as you know.)

"I'm glad you are keeping the door closed," she said. "It will keep the cats off your bed; they put fur all over it, as I have told you a thousand times."

A thousand times! Mummy does exaggerate sometimes, I thought.

I wondered whether Mummy and William had also been frozen, without moving, when I blew my whistle.

I would need to try it out again later.

"Now, Daddy has some exciting news for us," Mummy said.

"I have," he replied. "I have booked a summer holiday for us all; we are going to Disney World in Florida, in America. We will be there for ten days, which should give us enough time to see everything in the resort."

Well, we were excited. What a treat to look forward to, and the school holidays were only two weeks away.

I did know, though, that when I was looking forward to something, time went slower. *It would be better not blow my whistle too often, or it would take longer still*, I thought.

Monday and Back to School

I liked school, particularly seeing all my friends. But the weekends were definitely better, although they always seem to come to an end much too quickly.

William was now five and had just started at my school; I was in the third year.

We both went on the school bus together, which passed right outside our house, so it was very handy.

That was true provided we were outside and ready in good time, because the bus didn't stop if we were not standing there waiting outside the house.

We had missed the bus a couple of times, which made Mummy cross. Then she had to drive us in her car.

She hated doing it because there was never anywhere to park near the school. She said too many parents drive their children, even those who live close by and could easily walk—the older ones, anyway.

So Monday it was, and we were going back to school.

We just caught the bus by the skin of our teeth, as William was late getting dressed as usual. He was hopeless in the mornings, with no sense of time at all.

I went into my class, and he went off to his.

Today we were having a quiz in my class. It was general knowledge this week.

I was okay at this, but there were two children who usually beat me. I hated coming second or third.

I was determined to come first this week.

I was ready; I had a secret weapon, my magic whistle.

The first question came. "What is the highest mountain in the UK?"

I put my hand up and said, "Snowdon!"

My teacher started to say, "No—"

I blew my whistle.

She immediately stopped speaking and froze; everyone did. I went to the front of the class behind her desk and looked at the right answer.

I sat down and blew the whistle again. Then I said, "No, I mean Ben Nevis."

"Well done, Paul," she said. "That is correct."

I think this whistle is going to be very useful, I thought.

Later, after several more questions for which I chose to steal a few answers, we went to the next lesson.

I was the winner today, but nobody knew how I had suddenly become so clever.

The next lesson was arithmetic. I liked that because my daddy had taught me well on it. He had passed exams on this subject and was very good at it.

After that lesson, we went out to have our lunch.

Some children had the school meals. I hated them, especially the lumpy mashed potatoes.

I took my mum's homemade sandwiches and fresh fruit to finish. It was so much better.

After lunch the afternoon was to be a games day.

This week it was football. This was not one I liked very much, because I wasn't very good at it. Daddy said I have two left feet.

In our school our year was divided into two groups, called "houses." Mine was the Hornets; the other was the Buzzards. In football we were quite well matched, so both teams had a chance of winning.

Today, both of our teams scored one goal each in the first half, so it was all to play for after the ten-minute break for orange slices.

Each half was twenty minutes. After fifteen minutes of the second half had elapsed, there were no further goals. But then a chance came—and it was mine!

I ran past two defenders and scored a goal. I was over the moon! It was my first of the year. I was the hero who took our team to victory that day.

When I got home, I would have exciting news for Mummy and Daddy. I won at both the quiz and the football. What a day!

My Magic Whistle Gets Tested Again

Tea that day was one of my favourites—roast chicken, peas, mashed potato (without lumps), and gravy.

I was hungry and cleaned my plate. William did too, except he ate his twice as quickly as the rest of us, as usual. Daddy said he ate too quickly and should chew his food properly. William didn't take any notice, however; every mealtime was the same with him.

After we had finished, I went to my room with a mission in mind—to try out the magic whistle again.

I took it out and went back downstairs to the lounge, where Mummy and Daddy were watching a nature program on television. It was a program they watched every week.

William wasn't there; he was in his room playing on his rocking horse. It was made of metal and was very noisy.

I stood behind the sofa that Mummy and Daddy were sitting on and gently blew my whistle.

Instantly everything in the room froze—Mummy, Daddy, the dog, and the television too!

The only sound was William's metal rocking horse banging to and fro in his bedroom upstairs.

I blew the whistle again, and everything carried on as if nothing had happened. Mummy and Daddy had no idea I was even there behind them. I crept out having learnt something.

Only things near to me or things I could see would freeze when I blew the whistle. William was clearly out of range of this magic.

Crossing Off the Days

The next few days seemed to drag by slowly and without much happening.

Both William and I were excitedly looking forward to our holiday to Florida in America.

Daddy told us to expect it to be very warm and sunny throughout the holiday—most unlike the rain we had suffered for the past few days in England.

I had wanted to go out into the garden and woods to look for my seashell, the magic one that I told you about in my last adventure.

Mackie, our dog, had run off with it in her mouth. I had searched hard for it, but there was no sign of it.

I had to assume she had buried it, like she usually did with bones whenever she got them.

Because of the rain, I went up to my room and opened up the new jigsaw Mummy had bought for me. It was a picture of a space rocket on its launching pad, and it had three hundred pieces.

I got all the pieces out and laid them the right way up on a large piece of wood Daddy had cut for me.

I learnt from my last jigsaw that the best method was to first find the four corners and put them in their right positions, spaced correctly.

Next I would sort out all the edge pieces and set about making the outside border. After that, the really difficult part of filling it all in would begin.

I was, however, a long way from that yet!

During the next couple of hours, I had the four corners and most of the edging in place.

I decided that was enough for one day and got undressed and ready for bed. I was very tired.

I didn't wake until almost nine o'clock. It was Saturday, so there was no school that day.

I got out of bed and looked out of my bedroom window and was very pleased to see the rain had gone and the sun was shining again.

After getting washed and dressed, I went downstairs to have some breakfast. On school days, William and I have breakfast with Mummy at a quarter to eight, to be ready to leave for school at half past. But on weekends, we come down when we are ready.

William had already had his breakfast and was on the swing in the back garden.

I decided on cornflakes. I liked it with ice-cold milk and a little sugar. I used to put a lot of sugar on, but Mummy stopped us from doing that. She had told us that too much sugar was bad for our teeth. I hated the dentist, so I was happy to cut my sugar down to keep my teeth in good order.

23

An Exciting Find

After I had finished my breakfast, I went out into the garden—not to play with William but to play with our lovely little puppy dog, Mackie.

I realised that with so much else going on, I had neglected her. I knew she missed my games with her.

She was still a puppy and most playful. She needed attention, but she was so very patient.

She seemed to smile at me as I took her outside and told her to come and play. She really understood me.

I threw her latest ball for her to chase and bring back. (The last one was either buried somewhere or ripped into bits.)

I threw it several times, and she brought it back. I say back, but it was just to my feet. As soon as I tried to take it from her, she ran off with it again.

It was a game of cat and mouse. I had to work fast and artfully to get it from her!

This was a game she really loved.

I threw the ball several times, but finally when I threw it too far, out of sight, she was gone for quite a while.

Finally, just when I thought it was lost, she appeared—not with the ball in her mouth as before, but with my missing magic seashell!

I thought it was lost forever, but no, here it was back again. I was so pleased.

The problem was, she just grinned at me with it between her shining white teeth. She wouldn't let me have it.

Whenever I went near her to grab it, she ran off again. To her, this was just a game. To me it was not.

I decided on a plan. I went indoors and got her one of the teeth-cleaning bones that she loved to chew.

I offered it to her, and she immediately dropped my seashell and grabbed the bone. She then ran off to bury this new prize, I suspected.

I didn't care. I had my magic seashell back once more.

My Magic Things

Now, as you might remember from my previous adventure, this magic seashell allowed me to hear animals speaking in English. So it was very exciting for me.

I was so disappointed when our puppy dog ran off with it a couple of weeks ago and probably buried it somewhere.

I thought it was lost forever!

But now it was back—just like my magic sunglasses. I had everything safely back in my grandfather's chest safely, where they belonged.

Now I would be able to have amazing adventures.

I had glasses that could see a friendly monster, a seashell that let me hear animals talking, and now a whistle that could freeze things around me.

I was going to have some fun!

Holiday Preparations

The day had nearly come! We would be off tomorrow for our holiday to Florida, America—Disney World!

I could honestly say neither my brother nor I had ever been so excited.

Not only had we never been to America, but we had never even been on an aeroplane before!

We were excited but also a bit anxious. Going up in the air might be frightening.

Daddy, who had been on many planes before, assured us it was not only safe but also great fun.

We trusted him, so we tried to be calm and relax before our new adventure holiday.

Mummy helped us pack our bags and agreed to let me pack my magic things too.

She explained that there was a strict limit on how much luggage we would be allowed to take on board.

There was one thing about going away on this holiday that I didn't like. That was leaving our pets behind.

Our next-door neighbour, Mrs Kent, was going to come in each day and feed the cats and make sure they had enough water. There was a cat flap in the back door, so they could come and go as they wanted as usual.

Mackie, our puppy, was going to stay at my Uncle Norman's house nearby. He had a small dog of his own called Charlie. They had been together several times before, and they got along well together.

There was a very big, well-fenced back garden at his house, bigger than ours, so she would have plenty of places to play and bury things.

My uncle loved animals, and although I would miss Mackie, I knew she would be well cared for.

Florida, Here We Come!

We were up early in the morning in order to be in good time for our nine-thirty flight.

Daddy explained that we had to be at the airport two hours before, in order to check in our luggage and secure our seats.

We skipped breakfast, as we were going to eat some at the airport while we were waiting for the plane to be prepared and loaded.

We dropped off Mackie at Uncle Norman's, along with her bed, feeding bowls, and toys.

After a short drive, we arrived at the airport at 7.15. Daddy dropped us at the departure area and went to park the car in the long-term car park, where it would be safe for the ten days we would be away.

He was soon back and with us in the queue for the check-in desk. I now could see why we had to be there so early. There were more than a hundred people already in the line in front of us, all off to their holidays in Florida, all waiting for their seats.

It was here that we handed over Mummy and Daddy's big cases to be put into the plane's luggage hold—rather like the boot in a car.

I remember thinking how big it must be to hold over one hundred cases!

William and I only had small ones, which would fit under our seats, Mummy had explained.

After eating some breakfast in the café, we went through into the departure lounge. It was very big, with enough seats for everyone.

I looked out of the window, and there was our plane, being loaded with everyone's luggage. It was huge. It had two engines, one underneath each of the massive front wings.

Daddy explained that they were very powerful jets, made by a British company called Rolls Royce. He said this very proudly.

Finally a call came for us to get on board. My heart was pounding, and my knees were shaking!

We climbed up the stairs beside the plane and went inside. There were many rows of seats, three on each side of the gangway in the middle.

We found our seats, three on one side and one just across the gangway. William went in first and took a window seat. I went in next to him, and then Mummy sat next to the aisle, opposite Daddy.

Mummy explained that once we were flying, William and I could change seats as we wished so that we could both get the chance to look out of the window.

Soon we were ready for take-off. The captain told us all to fasten our seatbelts as a safety precaution.

This was just the same as when we were in our car at home. Nothing ever happened to need them, though.

We all fastened them up, and to make sure, the ladies looking after us, the flight attendants, walked up and down, checking.

The engines started up very loudly, and we raced down the runway at hundreds of miles an hour. Then the plane lifted off the runway, very smoothly, up into the clouds and then above them. Daddy had been right; it *was* fun—and really exciting.

During the seven-hour flight, we were first given a choice of drinks. William and I both had lemonade. It was okay but not as nice as Mummy's homemade.

Mummy had a coffee, and Daddy chose a beer. He explained that he had no more driving to do, and this was his holiday too! After a year of hard work, he told us all that he had earned it. Nobody disagreed with him.

After about two hours or so, they brought around hot meals for everyone. There was a choice of chicken, beef, or a vegetarian meal for those who didn't eat meat.

Mummy, William, and I all had the chicken. Daddy chose the beef. Our chicken dinner was very nice, but Daddy said his beef was a bit tough. He is spoilt at home because Mummy's cooking is always very good.

There was then a film to watch on little screens on the backs of the seats in front of us. We were given headphones to plug in to hear the sound. It was a Wild West cowboy film. None of us thought much of it.

I dozed off to sleep. The next thing I knew, we were all waking up to the captain telling us to fasten our seatbelts again for landing at Orlando International Airport.

The landing was quick and smooth. While we were up in the air, the plane didn't seem to be moving much at all. But as it got closer to the ground, it appeared to be going faster and faster.

Once it had stopped, it then turned and moved again, slowly now, towards the airport terminal where we would all get off.

After we left the plane, Mummy and Daddy collected their luggage, and then we boarded a massive bus to take us to our holiday hotel. It was only a short journey.

The hotel looked lovely, and it was actually inside Disney World. So, as Daddy had said, there would be no driving for him this holiday!

One thing we couldn't really understand or get used to was the time difference. We had arrived at just after four o'clock by my watch, after the seven-hour flight, but we had to set our watches back by eight hours to eight in the morning. So we had arrived before we had left.

Well, I didn't care or think about it too much; we were there, and the sun was shining. I remember thinking that if it was this warm first thing in the morning, how hot would it be later in the day?

Exploring Disney World

Well, the next few days were nothing short of amazing. This really was an incredible adventure land.

It was far bigger and better than anything we had ever seen before. Certainly nothing back home was like it. Truly, words cannot describe just how fantastic it was and how much we all enjoyed it.

It seemed to me that it was great fun for adults as well as children. I know for sure that Mummy and Daddy were very impressed with it all.

By the time we had spent several days exploring all the parks and had taken every ride we could, we were exhausted.

There were rides suited to all ages. Some were just beautiful; others were frighteningly fast and furious. So some were for older children and adults only.

There were still more than enough for us younger ones to enjoy.

41

The Wild Animal Park

Having seen and tried out every single corner of Disney's unbelievable adventure park, we went to see the famous Wild Animal Park nearby.

Just when we thought we couldn't be impressed any more than we had been already, we were blown away with the scale of this place. Animals from all over the world lived in huge, beautiful enclosures. They were so well looked after with plenty of space to roam. It really made our zoo back in England seem tiny.

I was spoilt now. Nothing would ever compete with this park.

The enclosure for the giraffes took twenty minutes just to walk around it. There were at least ten giraffes inside! I remembered that at home our zoo had just two.

A Frightening Experience

On our last day, we were still viewing all the wonderful animals in this park.

That day, we were in the big cats section. Lions, tigers, panthers, cheetahs—they were all there, each with their own enclosures.

It was when we were looking at the majestic lions that it happened.

There was suddenly screaming coming from the other side of the lions' enclosure. "My little girl is inside the safety fence," a woman screamed.

The noise and shouting from others were deafening.

I thought quickly and took my magic whistle from my pocket and blew it. Instantly, every person and every animal nearby froze!

I ran around top the other side of the enclosure to see if I could help.

I immediately saw the small girl, probably only about three years old, crouching on the floor just inside the lions' enclosure.

There were two huge lions approaching her close by, but both were thankfully frozen.

I could see what had happened straight away. There was a small gap in the bottom of the otherwise sturdy steel fence. It was far too small for the lions to get through, of course, but just big enough for an inquisitive small child to creep through.

The hole was too small for me, so there was only one option. I started climbing the steel fence. It was high and took quite a while. I thought, *I hope the whistle's spell doesn't have a time limit.*

Eventually I was over and inside the enclosure, looking at two ferocious lions just a few feet away!

I gently pushed the little girl back to the safety of the other side of the fence. This wasn't too difficult because she was as stiff as a board.

What was difficult, however, was climbing back over to safety myself. I managed it, though.

I ran back to where my family was and blew my whistle again. Immediately everything returned to normal.

No one knew what had happened.

The mother shouted, "She's back out! It's a miracle. She has escaped through that hole in the fence again."

Everyone was overjoyed—except perhaps the lions, who must have wondered where their tasty meal had gone.

Mummy said that the mother should have been taking better care of her daughter, and Daddy added that they should report the fault in the fence to be sure it was quickly repaired; otherwise something like this could happen again.

I agreed, knowing that I wouldn't be there to help if it reoccurred.

We had all had enough excitement for one day, so we set off back to our hotel to pack for our flight home in the morning.

Back Home Again

The journey home was uneventful, every bit as smooth and comfortable as the journey out.

It did seem strange changing our watches back again, though, having only just got used to the time difference.

I say it was uneventful, and it was—until we went to collect our luggage on arrival at the London airport.

We had all bought several souvenirs in America, so my small case now weighed too much to take on the plane and keep with me under my seat. I had had to put it into the hold with the adults' luggage.

It was when we were waiting for it all that the shock came. Mummy and Daddy's luggage appeared on the carousel with *everyone else's*—but not mine!

It seemed to have got lost somehow.

Daddy discussed it with the airport staff and filled out a lost luggage report.

They assured him that we needn't worry; they explained that sometimes cases get separated and go to the wrong airport.

They said they thought it would return, but if not, they would pay back the cost of the lost clothes.

Lost clothes! The clothes might have been Mummy's worry, but they weren't mine. My magic things could never be replaced with money.

If they didn't turn up, I would have no more adventures to tell you about.

It was a wonderful holiday, but it had a sad end for me at the moment. I just had to hope that my case would be found eventually and that I would have more adventures to tell you about. Keep your fingers crossed, please.

Printed in the United States
by Baker & Taylor Publisher Services